100 THINGS

by Masayuki Sebe

GECKO PRESS

Here are **100** mice.

How many are brown?

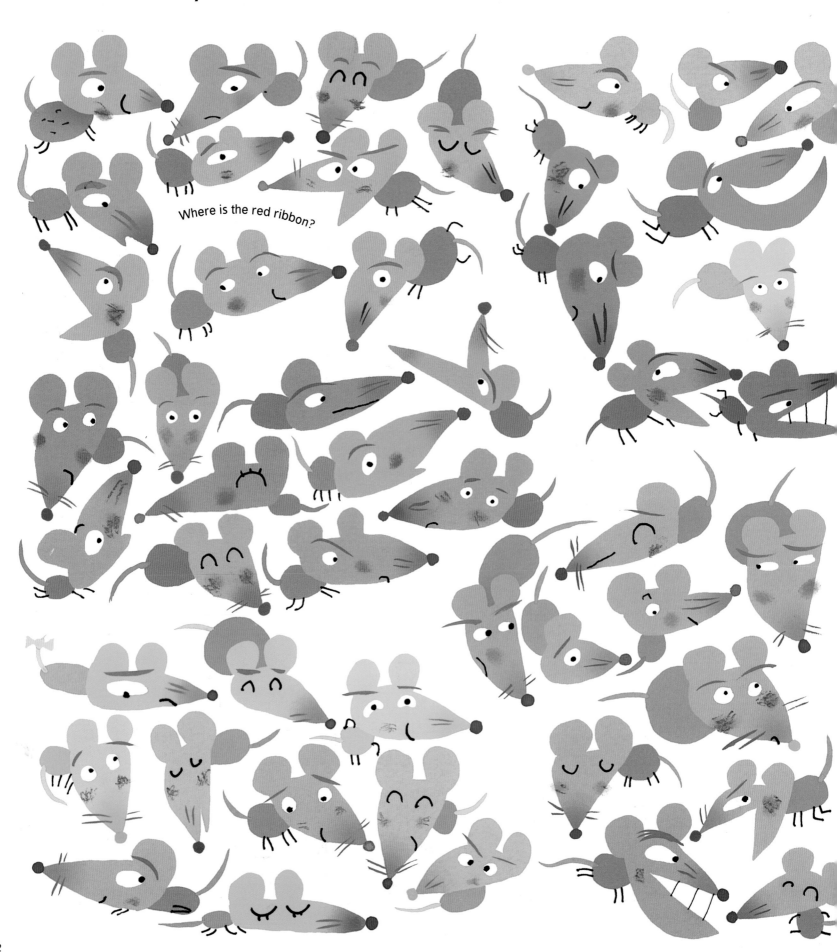

Where is the red ribbon?

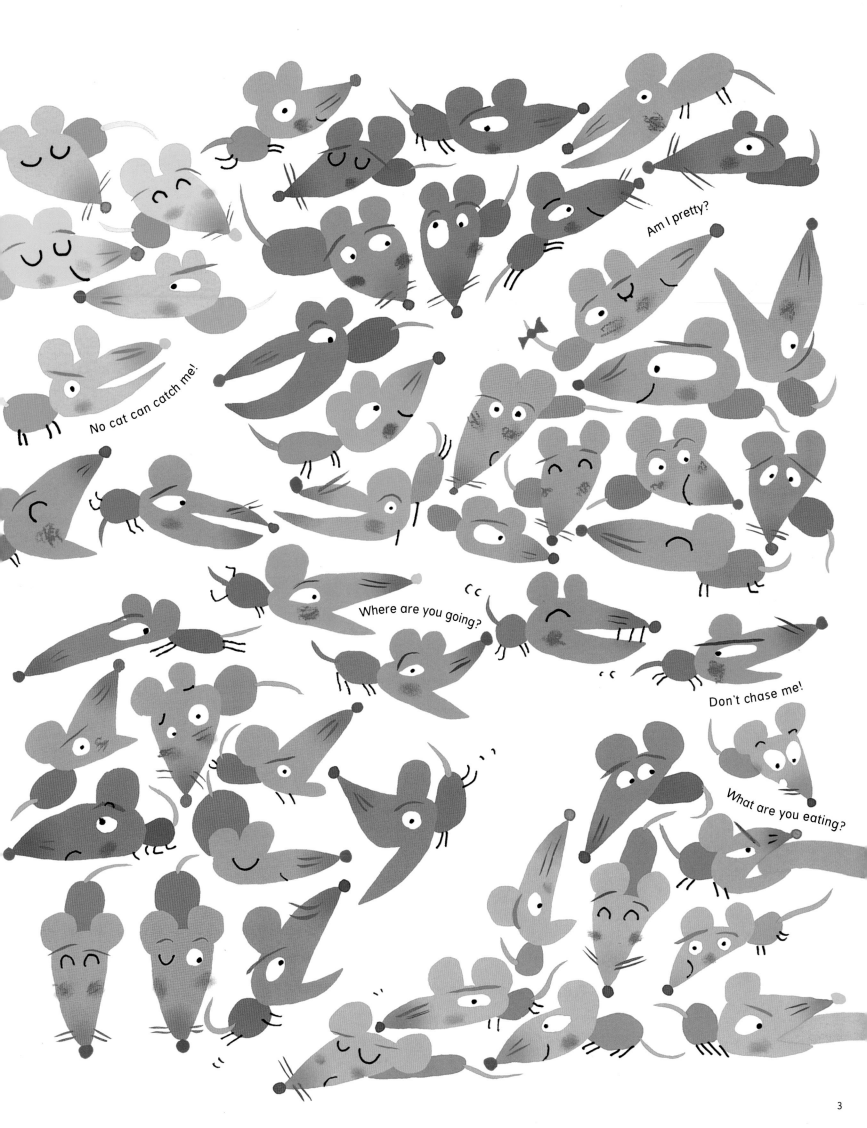

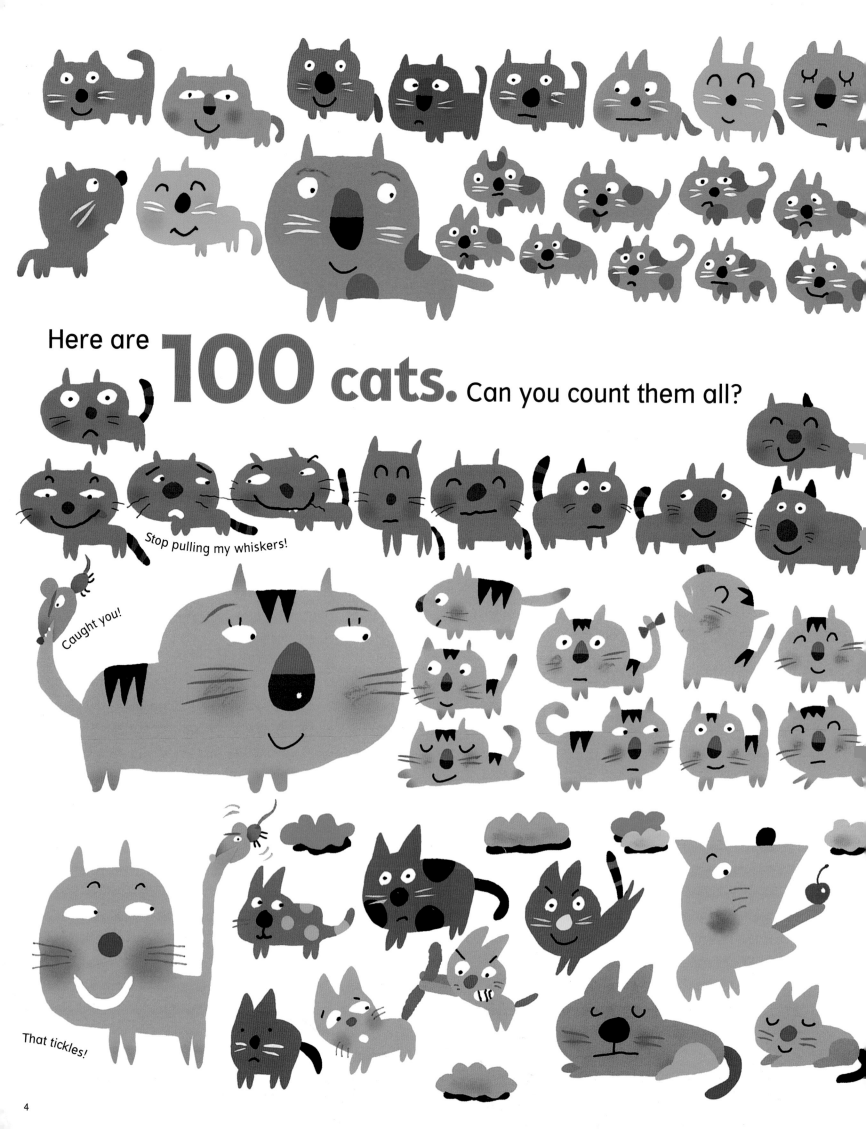

Here are **100 cats.** Can you count them all?

Stop pulling my whiskers!

Caught you!

That tickles!

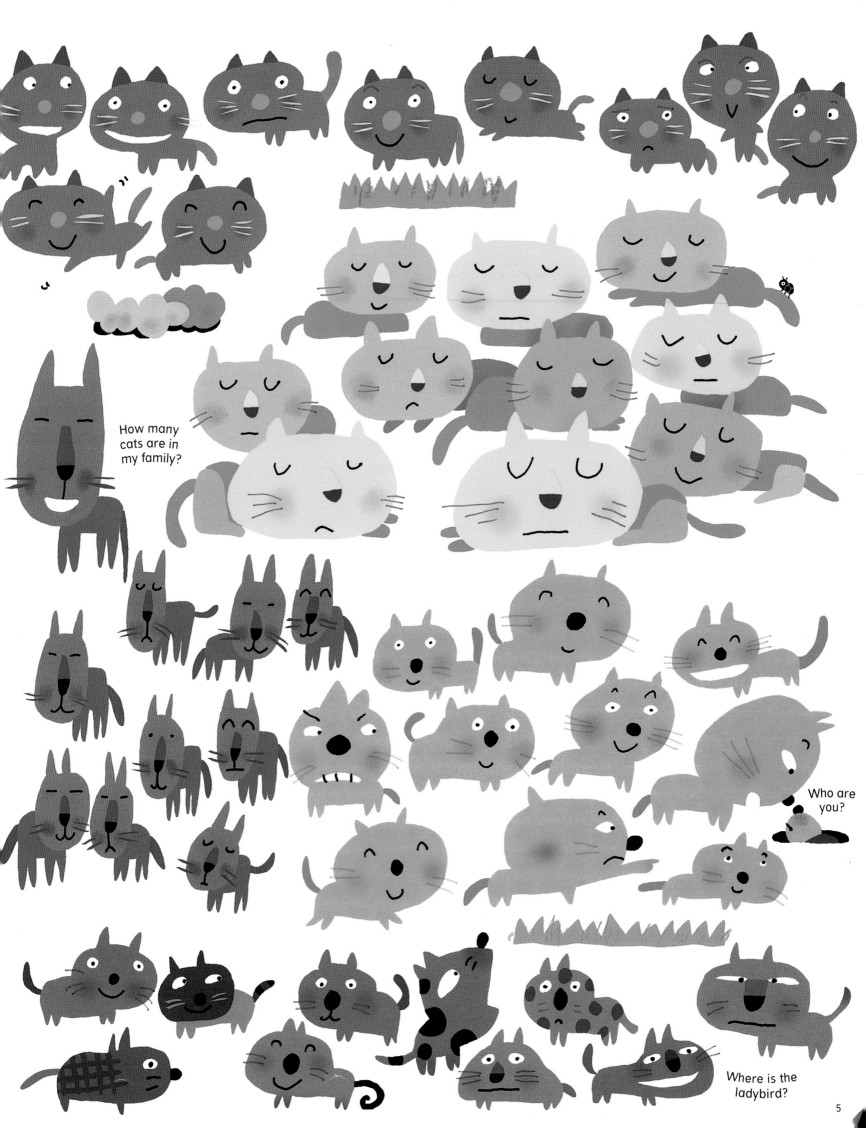

How many cats are in my family?

Who are you?

Where is the ladybird?

5

Here are **100**

What's that?

Stop it!

It stinks!

It stinks!

I feel much better now.

Heave-ho!

Is that an avalanche?

moles underground.

Hello.

Get out of my way!

That smells beautiful.

Where are we going?

Here are 100 sheep.

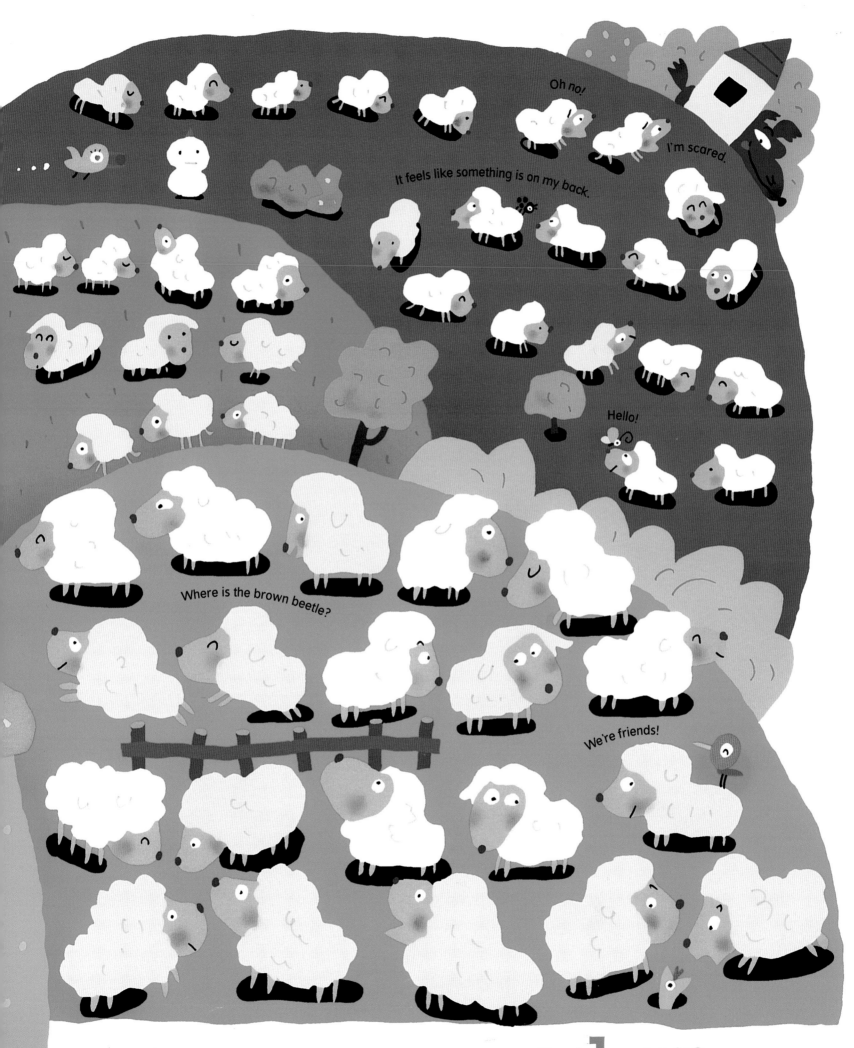

Can you find **1 rabbit?**

Here are **100 birds**

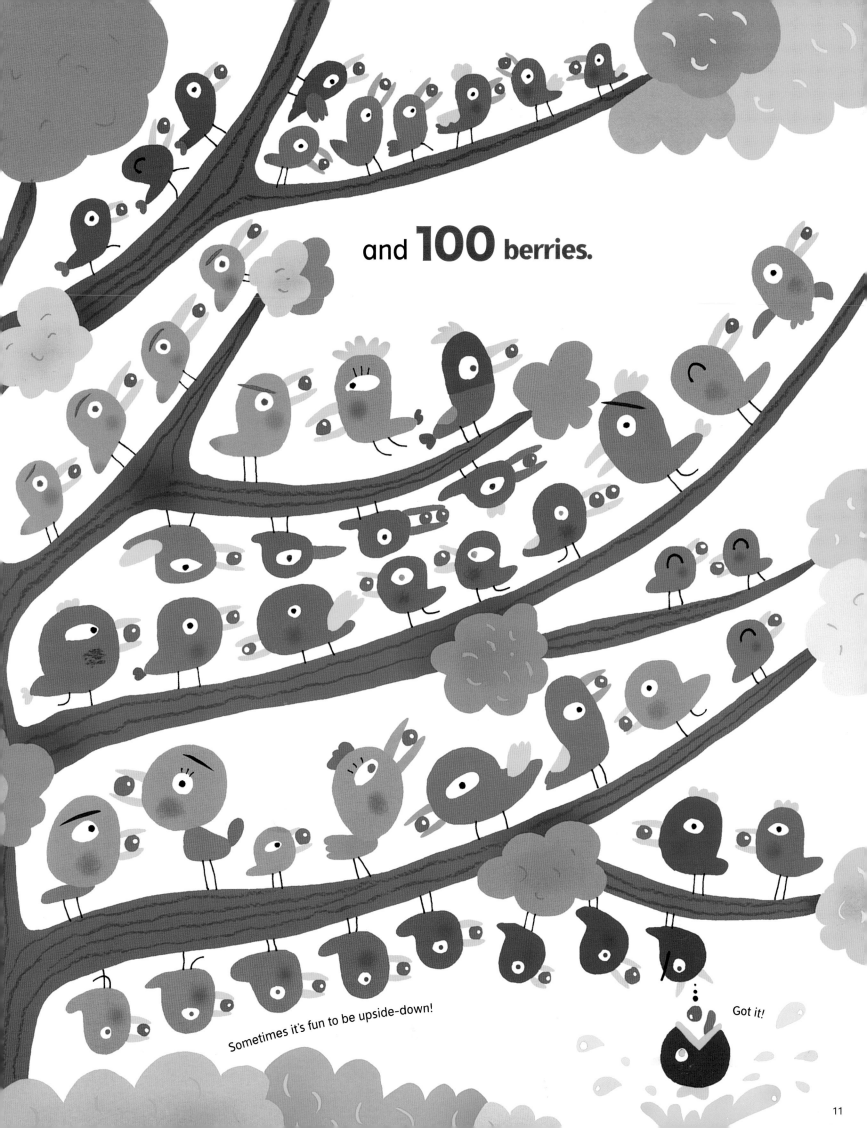

and **100** berries.

Sometimes it's fun to be upside-down!

Got it!

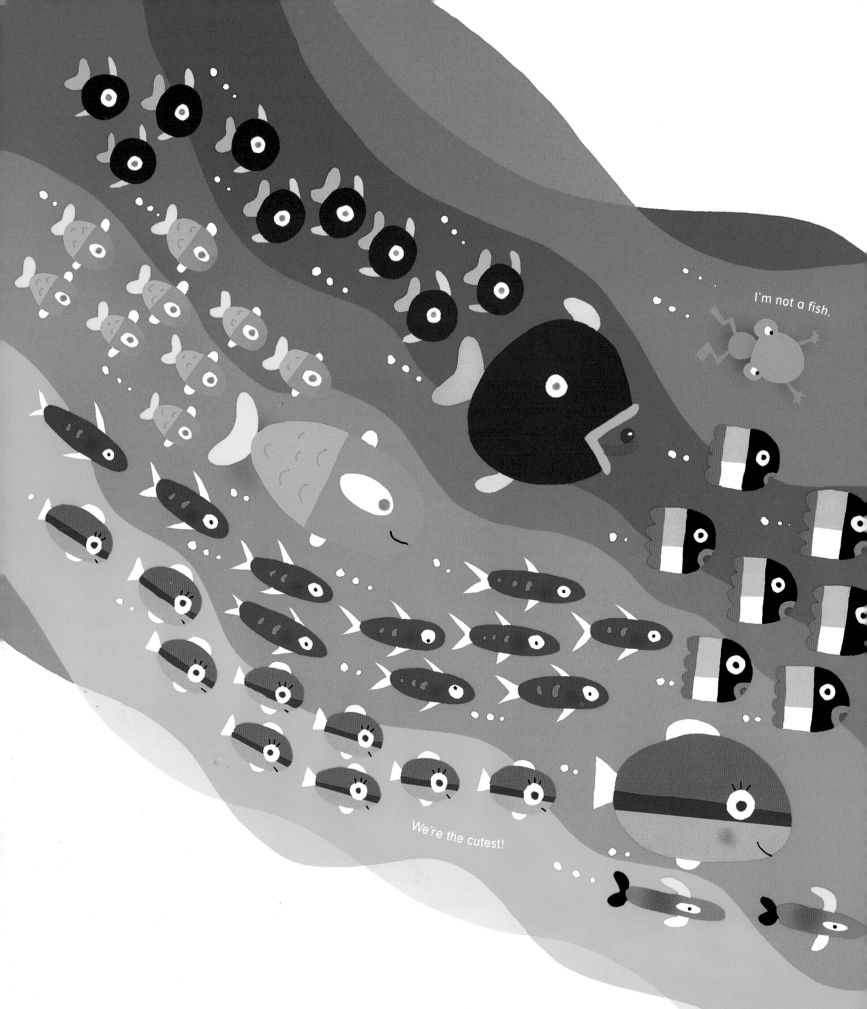

Here are **100** fish.

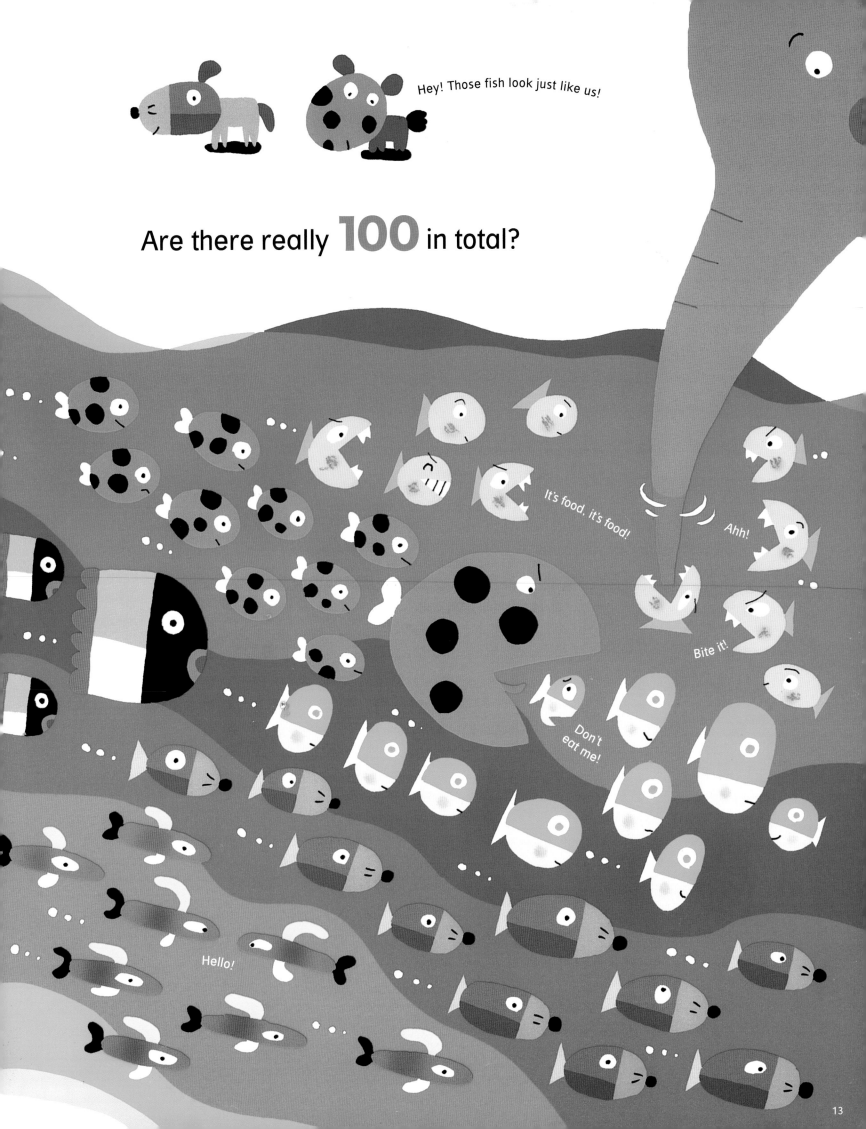

Are there really **100** in total?

elephants.

That looks delicious.

Here are **100**

Croak croak.

children.

Wow!

How many children are standing on their hands?

How many apples are there?

17

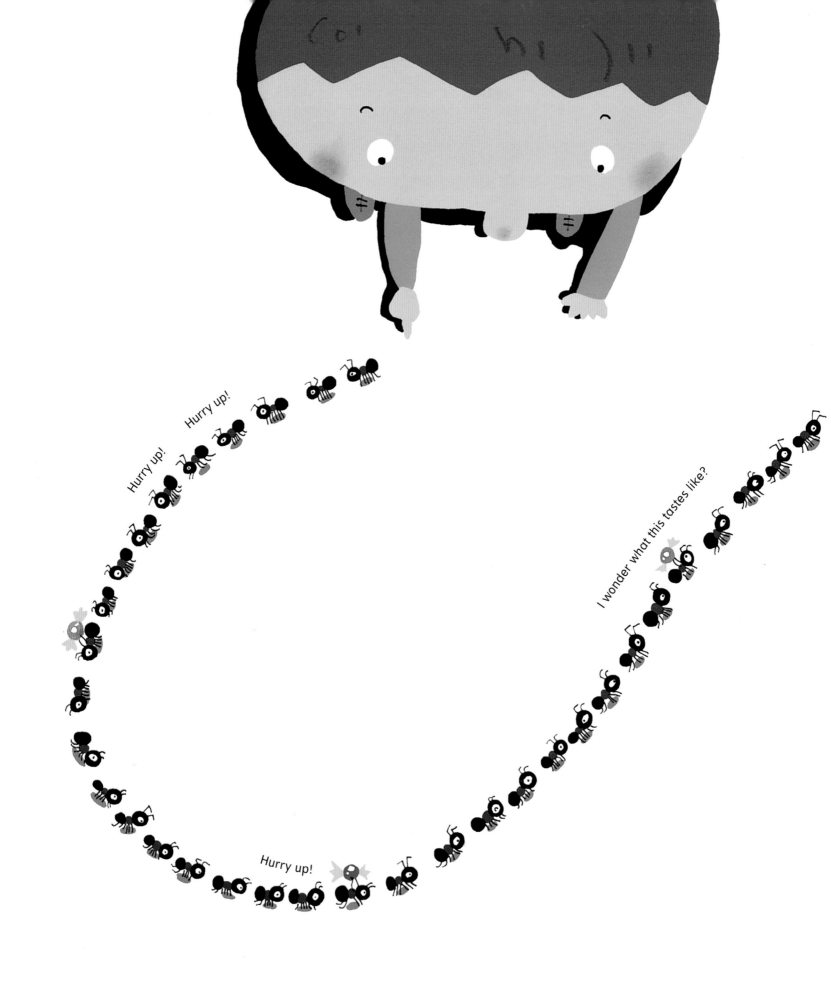

Here are **100 ants.**

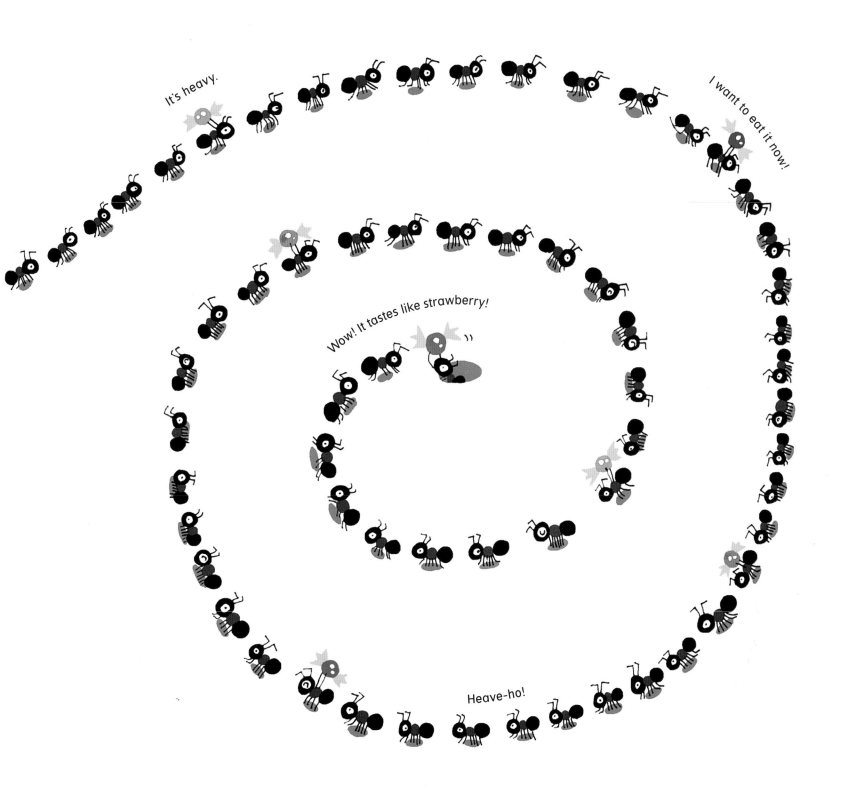

It's heavy.

I want to eat it now!

Wow! It tastes like strawberry!

Heave-ho!

I found a big one!

Are there really 100?

I want to eat a carrot. Can you find one?

Let's play!

Here are **100** cars

Beep! Beep!

Whee-ooh!

Whee-ooh!

I want to eat a watermelon. Can you find one?

and **100** houses.

Here are **10** mice, **10** cats, **10** moles, **10** sheep, **10** birds, **10** fish, **10** elephants, **10** children, **10** ants, and **10** houses.

100 things!

Hey!

What?

Wow, a cat!

Hurry up! Hurry up!

Where is the mouse
with the yellow ribbon?

(See pages 2–3)

Where is this cat?

(See pages 4–5)

Which mole farted?

(See pages 6–7)

Where is the
snowman?

(See pages 8–9)

Where is this bird?

(See pages 10–11)

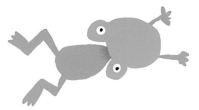

Where is this frog?

(See pages 12–13)

Where is the
elephant holding a
pineapple?

(See pages 14–15)

Who is wearing
this hat?

(See pages 16–17)

Where is the girl
putting a strawberry
on her head?

(See pages 16–17)

Where is the boy
cuddling this cat?

(See pages 16–17)

Where is this
sleeping ant?

(See pages 18–19)

Who lives in this house?

(See pages 20–21)

Where is this house?

(See pages 20–21)

Where is this truck?

(See pages 20–21)

This edition first published in 2011 by Gecko Press
PO Box 9335, Marion Square, Wellington 6141, New Zealand
info@geckopress.com

Reprinted 2012, 2013, 2014

English language edition © Gecko Press Ltd 2010

Original title: Kazoetegoran Zembu de 100
© 2008 by Masayuki Sebe
First published in Japan in 2008 by Kaisei-Sha Publishing Co., Ltd.
English translation rights arranged with Kaisei-Sha Publishing Co., Ltd.
through Japan Foreign-Rights Centre

A catalogue record for this book is available from
the National Library of New Zealand.

Typesetting by Luke Kelly, New Zealand
Printed by Everbest, China

ISBN hardback: 978-1-877467-81-3
ISBN paperback: 978-1-877467-82-0

For more curiously good books, visit www.geckopress.com